The Tricky Garden

CHARACTERS

Coyote
trickster

Bear
bully

Carrot
happy vegetable

Celery
happy vegetable

Lettuce
happy vegetable

SETTING

A garden

Coyote: Hello, Bear. What are you eating?

Bear: Berries. They're so tasty!

Coyote: May I have some?

Bear: No! I found this berry bush. I will eat all the berries!

Coyote: *(to audience)* Bear is so mean and selfish. He won't share. I am going to teach him a lesson. *(to Bear)* Bear, let's plant a garden together.

Bear: What's in it for me?

Coyote: A lot. You will get everything that grows above the ground. I will get everything that grows below the ground.

Bear: You will eat stuff that grows in the dirt? Yuck! I'll take that deal.

Coyote: Good. Let's plant carrots.

Bear: Yes! I love carrots!

Carrot: So Bear and Coyote plant carrot seeds. They water the carrot seeds.

Coyote: The light from the sun helps the seeds grow.

Carrot: After a few months, Bear and Coyote pull me out of the ground. For I am a carrot!

Bear: Yum! I love carrots!

Carrot: I do taste good. You can eat me raw or cooked.

Bear: Or in carrot cake!

Coyote: But Bear, what will you make with the green tops of the carrot that grow above the ground?

Carrot: Not much.

Bear: The green tops are yucky!

Carrot: Who are you calling yucky?

Bear: I want to eat the orange part of the carrot.

Coyote: That's the root. It grows under the ground. So I will get all the tasty carrot roots.

Carrot: Silly Bear!

Bear: Coyote, you tricked me. I want to plant a new crop. This time, I will take the roots that grow under the ground. You can have what grows above the ground.

Coyote: You mean the stems of the plant?

Bear: Sure.

Coyote: Okay, I'll take the stems. Let's plant celery.

Bear: Yes! I love celery!

Celery: So, Bear and Coyote plant celery seeds. They water the seeds. The sun shines.

Coyote: Our new crop is growing tall.

Celery: My stem grows thick. After many weeks, I am ready to be eaten. For I am celery!

Bear: Yum! Crispy, crunchy celery.

Celery: I taste great when I'm chopped up in salad, and I make a healthy drink.

Bear: I love celery with peanut butter.

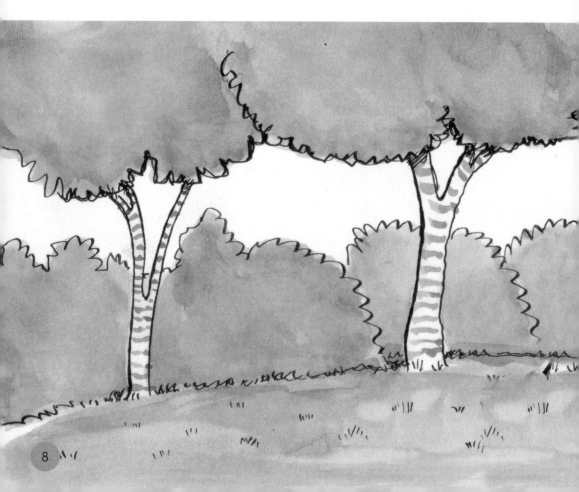

Coyote: I hope you love celery roots with peanut butter.

Celery: But my roots are not tasty. It is my *stem* that is good to eat.

Coyote: And I get the yummy celery stem. It grows above the ground.

Celery: Sorry, Bear.

Bear: This is not fair! I want to plant a new crop again. I want the stems that grow above the ground. I want the roots that grow below the ground, too.

Coyote: Okay. How about something green that makes a good salad?

Bear: Do you mean lettuce? I love lettuce!

Lettuce: So, Bear and Coyote plant lettuce seeds.

Coyote: We water the seeds.

Lettuce: The sun shines.

Bear: Our new crop is growing a big, fat head.

Lettuce: My leaves are full. I am ready to be eaten. For I am lettuce!

Bear: Yum! Lettuce! I love it in salads.

Lettuce: And don't forget about putting a leaf of me on a sandwich.

Bear: That is tasty, too.

Coyote: Too bad lettuce *roots* and lettuce *stems* do not taste good in a sandwich.

Lettuce: That is true. But why eat my roots and stems?

Coyote: We made a deal. Bear gets the roots and the stems.

Lettuce: But it is only my leaves that are good to eat.

Bear: That's not fair! You tricked me again, Coyote!

Coyote: Yes, I did trick you. And all this tricking is making me hungry. Now I must go home and cook all this good food.

Bear: You have so much food. I have none. Will you share your food with me?

Coyote: Why should I? You would not share your berries.

Bear: I'm sorry. It was selfish of me not to share my berries.

Coyote: Do you mean that?

Bear: Yes. I will go pick berries right now and share them with you. In fact, I will share my berries with all the animals.

Coyote: Then I will share my food, too. We'll have a harvest picnic. Everyone can come and share.

Bear: Thanks for being a good friend, Coyote. I love picnics!

Carrot, Celery, and **Lettuce:** Food tastes better when friends enjoy it together.

The End